KU-103-521

This Topsy and Tim
book belongs to

_____

Topsy + Tim

and the new baby

Jean and Gareth Adamson

Ladybird

All Ladybird books are available at most bookshops, supermarkets
and newsagents, or can be ordered direct from:
Ladybird Postal Sales PO Box 133 Paignton TQ3 2YP England
Telephone: (+44) 01803 554761 *Fax:* (+44) 01803 663394

A catalogue record for this book is available from the British Library

Published by Ladybird Books Ltd
A subsidiary of the Penguin Group
A Pearson Company

© Jean and Gareth Adamson MCMXCV
This edition MCMXCVIII

The moral rights of the author/illustrator have been asserted
LADYBIRD and the device of a Ladybird are trademarks of Ladybird Books Ltd Loughborough Leicestershire UK

*All rights reserved. No part of this publication may be reproduced, stored in a retrieval system, or transmitted in any form or
by any means, electronic, mechanical, photocopying, recording or otherwise, without the prior consent of the copyright owner.*

Topsy and Tim were having tea with
Tony Welch. Tony's mum was going to
have a baby. It was growing in her
tummy.

Tony put his hand on his mum's big tummy. 'I can feel the baby moving,' he said. Tony's mum let Topsy and Tim feel her tummy too. 'Ooh!' said Topsy. 'It kicked my hand.'

'When will the baby be born?' asked Tim.
'In a week or so,' said Tony's mum.
'I hope it's a girl,' said Topsy.

Later, Tony took Topsy and Tim upstairs to see the new baby's bedroom. 'I'm going to let it sleep in my old cot,' he said.

Topsy and Tim had brought a bag
of their old baby clothes for the
new baby. They helped Tony's mum
to put the clothes away in a drawer.

One morning, Tony came to school
looking very pleased. 'I've got a
baby brother,' he told the class.
'He was born in the night and he's
called Jack.'
'You are lucky,' said Topsy and Tim.
'Yes,' said Tony. 'I haven't seen him
yet because he was born in hospital
but Daddy is taking me there after school.'

The next day, Tony came to play
with Topsy and Tim. He was carrying
a new car.
'Jack gave it to me,' he told them.
'Can we see Jack?' asked Tim.

'We'll go and meet Jack next week,'
said Mummy, 'when Tony's mum
brings him home.'
'What's he like?' asked Topsy.
'He's very little and he cries a lot,'
said Tony.

Topsy and Tim talked about Jack
all week long. When Saturday came,
Mummy took them to see him.

'Can I hold him?' asked Topsy.
She sat on the floor and Tony's mum
put him on her lap. He felt very warm.
'I want to hold him, too,' said Tim.

Jack began to cry. Tony's mum
picked him up.
'Why is he crying?' asked Tim.
'Babies don't know how to talk,
so they cry when they need something,'
said Tony's mum.

'He's pooed his pants,' said Tony.
'No, he hasn't,' said his mum.
'Perhaps he's hungry,' said Topsy.
'I think you're right,' said Tony's mum.

Tony's mum started to feed Jack.
He stopped crying and made loud
sucking noises.
'I want a drink, too,' said Tony.

'There are some cartons of juice
in the fridge, Tony,' said his mum.
'I expect Topsy and Tim would like
a drink too.'

After they'd finished their drinks,
Topsy and Tim and Tony went
to play football in the garden.

When they came back in, Tony's mum was changing Jack's nappy. Topsy and Tim stood and watched.

'Now I'm going to give Jack his bath,'
said Tony's mum. 'Would you like to
help me, Tony?'
Tony shook his head.

Topsy and Tim played with Jack
while Tony's mum put warm water
in the baby bath and tested it
with her elbow to make sure it was
not too hot for Jack.

When she put Jack in the bath, he began to cry.
'He doesn't like the water,' said Tim.
'Yes, he does,' said Tony. He lifted the baby's sponge and squeezed some water on to Jack's toes.
Jack stopped crying and gurgled.

'He's laughing,' said Topsy.
'That's because he likes his big
brother,' said Tony's mum and
she gave Tony a hug.

'Isn't Tony lucky to have a little
brother,' said Topsy on the way home.
'I think Jack's lucky to have a
big brother like Tony,' said Tim.